SPANISH POTTERY
AND OTHER STORIES

SHEILA COHEN

To Margaret,
love from Sheila.

Born in Glasgow and now based in Suffolk, Sheila Cohen spent most of her working life as a teacher and careers adviser. Throughout her career, however, she pursued her own writing and art, recording thoughts and ideas, and sketching people and places. Since retiring in 2009, she's devoted herself to these pursuits, taking creative writing and drawing classes, producing a series of pastels and watercolours and publishing a self-help book sharing learnings from across her career. *Spanish Pottery* is her first collection of short stories.

Also by Sheila Cohen

How to Have a Great Day Off

This short book lets you into a little secret. If you take a day off work, or you have a quiet weekend to yourself, you'll get more out of it if you organise it properly – even if what you need from the day is to do nothing at all. This book – with witty examples and anecdotes woven through its pages – shows you how to do it, for a day off that's exactly what you need it to be.

Amazon Publishing, 2014.
Kindle or Print Editions

For Maurice

Published by Kindle Direct Publishing, 2018

Copyright © Sheila Cohen, 2018

The characters in this book are fictitious. Any similarity to real persons, living or dead, is coincidental and not intended by the author.

ISBN: 978-1724812391

Cover design: *Azulejos* glazed tiles – Goran Bogicevic

Printed by Amazon

CONTENTS

Spanish Pottery
9

Finished Business
23

Across the Road
35

Red Bikini
45

Girl in a Hurry
57

Two Girls
69

Do Well, Go Far
79

The Holy Family
97

Warriors
109

The Visitor
125

Acknowledgements
136

Spanish Pottery

Spanish Pottery

'Did you apply for the teaching job?' Martin asks.

'No,' says Angela, stirring the cheese sauce, 'I'm not quite sure I want to.'

Martin is exasperated. 'Look, we've discussed this. When I come home from work you seem to be getting more and more unhappy every day.'

'I know. I'm sorry. I'm not sure I want to go back into school yet, but I need to be working at *something*. I thought moving to the country might be a chance to explore other directions.'

'So what's stopping you? You know I'm on your side whatever you choose to do. You're doing well in your art class – is that what you want to develop?'

'Sometimes I think it is.'

'What does your tutor say? She sells her own work, doesn't she?'

'Yes. And she thinks I'm good, but it's common knowledge that you have to have a studio.'

Daniel comes into the kitchen to ask if dinner's

ready. 'Yes. Tell Colin, and go and wash your hands,' says Angela.

'Let's look at it again this weekend,' Martin says as the boys take their seats at the table.

Angela asks them what went on in school today. Daniel is busy poking about in his cheese sauce to remove the cauliflower.

'We had Mrs Jarrold's mince,' says Colin between mouthfuls of fish-finger and potatoes. 'It was *de*-licious.'

'Don't be silly, she meant what did you *learn,*' says Daniel. 'I learnt about mini-beasts. Oh, and I've got *terrible* art homework to do. Mum, will you help me?'

Angela feels relieved. She can't think of anything nicer than helping her son with his art homework. That's what she'd done in London for 25 years, help kids learn. She'd been a Primary teacher with Art as her specialist subject, but recently both she and Martin had felt stale in their jobs and neither had been able to get promotion. Several friends had moved out to the country and reported their quality of life vastly improved, so they'd followed suit and here they were. Martin had quickly got a job and was enjoying it but Angela had given herself a year off to adjust to their village setting and get the house furnished. Although it's a period building, she's tried to bring as much light in as possible and bought old but plain furniture to keep a feeling of brightness and space. Now the interior is finished and the year is up.

She's got to know some mothers at the school gate. A couple of them are, like her, in their forties, but they are stay-at-home mums. It's not that Angela doesn't have *activities*, but in her mind they don't add up. She feels at a loose end most days, and last weekend was horrified to hear her status summed up by a male friend from London as *glorified housewife*.

Next morning, after taking the kids to school, Angela sweeps cereal bowls into the sink, bundles stray clothes away from the sofa, returns channel-changers, newspapers, school information sheets, crisp-packets to where they belong. Today, she's going with her friend Kate and Kate's old school friend Sarah to a Sale of Spanish Pottery at a house in the village. She looks at her watch – 10.45. She had so much to think about and now it's time to go. They meet outside the village shop.

On their way up the hill to the newer part of the village, there's a chill in the air. Kate says the cherry blossom is late this year. The soft yellow willow leaves droop waiting for warmth and Angela feels that any time they'll turn lime-green and summer will settle. Sarah's smiling, hands warm in her coat pockets. She seems glad to have company and somewhere to go.

'Would either of you be interested in a basket-weaving course at the Wildlife Centre?' asks Kate, whose husband runs the centre.

Sarah doesn't even answer. Angela says she'll think about it, but she won't.

'Oh, and there's a vacancy on the Parish Council. Angela?'

'No thanks, Kate. I'll stick to the school committee for now.'

Out in the country, Angela is aware of the danger of being drawn in to activities just to keep busy, which Kate does on an industrial scale – she runs the children's club on a Friday night, organises the September Village Breakfast, and is a Parent Governor of the school. She used to be a solicitor. Sarah, on the other hand, doesn't join anything. It's a mystery what she does all day.

Their destination appears on the left, set back from the road.

'Do we know who this lady is?' Sarah asks Kate.

'She's new. No children. Husband's a builder I think, which might explain the quick renovation.' Kate always knows what's going on in the village. In fact there's almost nothing she doesn't know.

This house, its *For Sale* sign at last taken down, is a plain, modern building, standing, newly painted, forlorn on a mound of earth. The slope up to it has now been laid with a single line of flagstones, with the fine shoots of a newly sown lawn on either side.

'Hello, I'm Nicola,' says the hostess, with a firm handshake. She's thin and energetic but a bit flustered and red in the face.

The kitchen is bright and spacious with the latest fittings and appliances. Angela sees a glint of enticement in Kate and Sarah's eyes. They would love to glide open the smooth cream drawers and peek into the wall-oven. Their own kitchens, with stoves, wooden dressers and deep sinks have become museums cluttered with all kinds of antiques – old cracked china, stoneware, brass and copper items collected over the years. On Nicola's high marble-topped breakfast-bar is an array of colourful Spanish glazed pots, bowls and plates. Accepting her offer of a cup of coffee, they begin to look over the merchandise.

'These are beautiful,' says Kate. 'I haven't seen this style of pottery around for a long time. How did you come by it?'

'It was while Trevor and I were in Spain looking for a place to renovate we noticed roadside outlets with pots on display and just couldn't resist buying lots to sell back home.'

Angela examines a flower-pot, turning it to see a pattern of olives and leaves, each one the result of a few single confident brush-strokes. She remembers the thrill of buying such lovely pieces on holiday in Spain years ago. It's going to be difficult to choose.

There are bowls with vast pink flowers, plates with cockerels, and huge platters painted with fish, birds, fruit.

'You haven't been here long, Nicola, have you?' asks Kate.

'Well, it's nearly a year now.'

'Did you move from far away?'

'No, from Essex, not that far.' Nicola bites her lip as if she were holding something back.

Just at that moment, they hear the front door opening and a scraping sound on the ceramic floor tiles. This must be Trevor. The women stop talking. He looks younger than Nicola, of medium build with a slight paunch and wavy sandy-coloured hair falling into his eyes, forehead beaded with sweat as he heaves a large cardboard box into the corner. He straightens up, grimaces across to the women and reminds Nicola that he won't be home till ten next morning, then rushes off again through the front door. Everyone is taken aback by his lack of friendliness, their eyes wide searching for an explanation.

Nicola folds her arms and smiles as she attempts to provide one. 'He's always in a hurry,' she says. 'Builders work late – if he's on a job far away, he sometimes stays over.'

Kate, who is good at conversation links, manages to find a way back to the pottery. 'And do *you* work, Nicola, I mean, apart from providing us with these lovely pots?'

'Yes. I've been helping Trev with the business. I do his books. That's how we met – I used to work for his father in the office and when Trev took over as manager I could see he needed help. One thing led to another,' she finishes, with even less of a smile than Trevor's.

'You've both done a really good job on the place,' says Angela. The other two murmur in agreement.

'Thank you. Yes, it has been non-stop.'

Kate chooses two egg-cups and Sarah's deciding on a plate for her sister 'who likes this kind of thing'. Angela has gathered a large fruit bowl, two plant pots, several plates all different, and wants that mug with the pale blue dolphin.

'Do you have a garden at the back as well?' asks Kate, curious as ever.

'Oh, yes, there's a long garden. Would you like to see it?' offers Nicola, getting up.

Angela's got used to the country habit of snooping around on Open Garden events during the summer. People stand admiring banks of sage and pink, clumps of yellow behind blue, prowl around winding paths with ferns and running water, sit at wrought-iron tables forking up slabs of coffee-cake with butter icing. Their own garden is big and wild, and since Martin limits himself to cutting the grass leaving her to become a servile weeder, not much progress is being made. Kate once took her to Sarah's place on the outskirts of the village one evening when the children were away at school camp. They drank white wine on her patio, but the garden was sad and abandoned, with overgrown bushes, worn grass and struggling flowers. Sarah seemed to have given up on it – in spite of the piles of *Gardeners' Weekly* on her cane table.

Nicola's back door opens on to another straight path leading to a shed through a well-cut lawn lined with red tulips. It's embarrassing walking up and back down when there is really nothing to look at. Back indoors they return to the table to pay for their purchases. Just to make conversation, Sarah asks if they are still working on parts of the house. Nicola looks uncomfortable.

'No, we're putting it up for sale actually. I'm afraid we're splitting up. It's OK,' she continues bravely. 'It's for the best. We've only just come to a decision.' She doesn't give signs that she wants to provide any further information.

After an uneasy silence, Kate says quietly, 'Well, sorry to hear that, Nicola.'

'I've got some carrier bags and cardboard you can have,' Nicola says, getting them out from a cupboard. After such bad news it's important not to rush off but to make the departure seem slow and relaxed by wrapping carefully, getting out money and cheque-books, fussing about change, looking at watches, talking about the weather. Angela is last to leave. She lingers, thanking Nicola and wishing her all the best.

'If you know anyone else who'd be interested in the pottery, please let them know.'

Angela says she will, and might even come back for some more for herself.

Looking as cheerful as she can, Nicola closes her new glass door.

'Wow! That was a spectacular situation,' says Angela, on the way back. 'Surely they'll change their minds, after having set all this up.'

'No,' says Kate. 'By the look of him, he's made up his mind. He looks to me like the kind of man who would never commit.'

'That's a quick judgement, Kate,' says Sarah. It may just be that they're not suited. She looks neurotic to me. Did you see the way she was wringing her hands? And she's obsessively tidy – I mean, that totally empty kitchen, the prim unromantic garden. He probably feels he has to escape.'

'Maybe, but look,' says Kate, getting fired up, 'he's usually home late and is not coming home tonight. It's so easy for him not to tell her exactly what he's up to from day to day or to make up a story. He's probably been seeing someone else.'

Sarah rounds on her. 'Hang on,' she says. 'My

Gerald works in London, gets home late, and often stays over. You have to trust your husband!'

Angela stays out of it. Kate and Sarah know each other very well, but a chasm has opened up between them. They walk in silence back to the shop. Angela, cradling her large brown paper bag, says she'll see them at the school gate. Distracted, the other two nod and go their separate ways.

Angela puts the carrier bag on the sofa in the lounge, where the sun slants in on her yellow ochre colour-scheme. She makes a cheese sandwich in the kitchen and brings it through, thinking about the dramatic events of the morning. Poor Nicola, all by herself, probably with no one to talk to, waiting for Trevor to come home only to rush off again. She'll be phoning her family and friends back in Essex. He won't be the one putting the house back on the market, unpicking everything they've established. She's courageous though, and efficient, has experience of working in a builder's office and when she gets untangled from Trevor she can get back into similar work.

Strange how this visit set off such an explosive disagreement about absentee husbands. Martin works nearby and she trusts him, doesn't think he's about to run off, but she feels uneasy just now being financially dependent on him. They've always earned equally. Even after having the children, she went quickly back to work. If she carries on like this she'll end up like Kate, solely involved with charitable activities, or like Sarah, sitting around all day doing nothing.

She rushes upstairs and hauls out dusty folders of art-work from under the bed in the spare room. Spreading over the floor her life drawings, self-portraits, pastels, abstracts, and still-lifes from A level and teacher-training, she's surrounded by a collage of colour and line, all her own. She dusts herself down and looks up at the shelf. Here in smaller notebooks she has taken with her on every holiday since she was a teenager are pencil and ink drawings of people sitting in town cafes, on beaches, church facades, statues – and she's proud of them.

Looking around, her new studio begins to be created in her mind. The bed can go. Maybe get a sofa bed. Filing-cabinet will fit under the stairs, buy art-storage drawers, build a surface for brushes and paints, easel in the corner. It'll be a start at least. Just try, and see how things go.

She looks at her watch – 3.15. How can it be that time already? When she gets to the school gate, all the children are out. Her boys run towards her.

'Mum, can we bring Harry and James home to play football?'

Angela agrees, nodding to their mum who says she'll collect them at five, if that's OK, but then tells the children to stand by the school gate for a just a minute while she talks to Kate.

Kate is gathering her own children but Sarah's son George is also with her. Angela goes over to her to ask where Sarah is.

'She needs time to cook dinner,' says Kate. 'Gerald's coming home early. He said there's something they have to talk about.'

Finished Business

Finished Business

Would anyone phone her tonight? At the Tube station that hot Friday evening in 1970, Janice crossed the tiled floor which marked the margin of the little patch of London she called home. End of year drinks with her student friends were behind her and what was ahead? Her summer holiday began alone. Head down to avoid sensing the plans of others, she knew of course there were couples everywhere with full shopping bags or already dressed to go out.

She opened the door of their rented basement flat, trying to think what she and Michael would normally have been doing on a Friday night. Michael had packed his things in her absence the week before and moved back home to North London, leaving, on the blue Formica table, his keys and his half of the rent.

She looked at the phone in the hall and considered calling home to Liverpool but decided to wait until things got even worse. It would be difficult to announce the break-up because although her mum had never said anything negative about the relationship Janice sensed she'd had no faith in it. The phone rang anyway.

Olaf spoke confidently. During his long visits to London when working alongside Michael, the three of them had often had a meal out together. Now that he came over from Sweden only for shorter trips, he needed company and perhaps she would too. He proposed coming over to the flat.

'Yes, tomorrow sounds fine,' said Janice automatically, relieved to have someone to talk to and something fixed for Saturday. She sat down on the lumpy sofa in the lounge. Olaf was so sensible and kind. His slow almost perfect English had sounded so comical at first. Would he be wearing that fine silky checked jacket? Imagine welcoming someone like him home every evening and slipping your arms around his waist under the jacket. Then she remembered the photo of his wife and children being pulled from the top pocket.

At least she had a date. She got up to explore what there was in the kitchen cupboard, and opened a tin of ravioli for dinner. Michael would not have permitted such low standards. The kitchen was dark and silent so she returned to the lounge to eat it. People passed by the railings above and the last rays of sunlight exposed the worst of the stains layered on the shabby powder-blue carpet which had been the minimum requirement to turn this unpromising basement into a basic dwelling. Lavinia, a friend on the course, had delivered it, tied up with a belt, on the back of her motor-bike, insisting that after being together for two years it was time the couple lived together, although Janice herself knew Michael was not keen. She swallowed the last forkful of ravioli with this memory.

The phone rang again. Janice could face her mum now. 'Sorry, who's that?' asked Janice.

'Charlie. From Skye,' replied a soft voice.

'Charlie-from-Skye?' repeated Janice in a daze.

'You came to our farm with your friend last summer.'

Janice recalled the two bedraggled girls at the farmhouse door, the tent on the waterlogged field, and later, *the pub which does not close.*

'Oh, *Charlie*, I remember. Of course! Where are you?'

'On someone's floor tonight, but I wondered if I could stay with you tomorrow night?'

'Yes, I think so,' she said, giving him the address, but took his number in case there was a problem.

Janice returned to the sofa. She hadn't expected to hear from Charlie again. He'd never left the island, although she had encouraged him to. These adventurous holidays! She loved to explore, but would have chosen to do so with Michael, if he had not been going on holiday with his family.

Now Janice had two relative strangers coming

to the flat the next day, one at three o'clock and the other at 7.30. This was an alternative to being alone but not at all what she wanted. Her first instinct was to run away, but where would she go? Then she remembered what usually happened on Friday nights – she would go home with Michael for their family meal. Just at this moment he'd be finishing his apple strudel, and here she was, with nothing better to do than go into their makeshift 'bedroom' all by herself, where the double mattress lay on the linoleum floor, and get ready for bed. Nothing else for it. It would be all right. She'd get up early, do some shopping and sort everything out.

But in the morning Janice was in a panic. She wondered how many more calls she'd get. Did people everywhere know she was now on her own? Had there been a public announcement?

The baker where they usually went for rye bread was closed. She found another shop and bought a packet of scones. Michael would have brought something from home. On the corner was a small supermarket where they'd gone to get cheese rolls to take in the van when his band travelled to gigs, bumping along uncomfortably in the back with the instruments, but the band had packed up since he'd 'gone straight' and got a good job. Once they'd been at a market somewhere and there was a photo of them both holding a lizard. Janice picked up a packet of ham. Michael would have wanted salami.

She sighed. The man at the till said, 'Can't be that bad!'

It was all a puzzle. He was easy to be with and *he* had pursued *her*, so why did she now have to go out looking for someone else? Back on the main road, she was at the place of the final parting. They'd been crawling along in his car in heavy traffic, and she'd finally asked him outright.

'Michael, do you think you could ever see us getting married and having children?'

'No,' he'd said quietly, 'I can't see that.'

The car stopped at the lights and she'd got out. Had she banged the door?

Olaf was waiting down the steps at the door at three o'clock exactly, looking a bit insecure. There was the jacket, smooth as ever. She made tea and he followed her around, mouth hanging slightly open as she bustled around to no particular effect. He'd been told by Michael of the break-up and they discussed it briefly but when the conversation dwindled Janice was nervous. Why hadn't she arranged to meet him somewhere else? He took her hand and led her to the 'bedroom'. She let herself be led, feeling nothing of her old attraction to him here in this damp-smelling room with no window. He stood holding out his arms for her and she stepped back and told him 'No.' Even as he stood at the door, ready to go, he put his arm round her in his fatherly way and bent his head to kiss her but she wriggled free, nimbly took hold of the door-catch and he was gone.

For a while she sat with her head in her hands, too confused even to cry, then made a cup of coffee and found an old chocolate biscuit in her handbag. She'd take Charlie out to a pub and have some food. In the bathroom, that hideous cracked mirror slyly displayed her anxious, frightened face. She heard the rumble of the trains underground and felt the motion of the crumbling floor under the worn lino. The bath water was yellow.

The bell rang at 7.30 and Charlie traipsed along the hall into the lounge where he and his back-pack came to rest on the sofa. His face was red with the sun. He looked taller and leaner but still had his shoulder-length curls.

In the pub it was clear he had no money. Janice sat down and gave him £5 to fetch drinks and tell her what was on the menu. They had beer and shepherd's pie.

'So what are you doing here in London?'

'Just exploring unknown territory, like you in Skye.'

'And what have you found?'

'That London's a bit much for me, Janice, but I'm glad I did it, because I feel I could manage to study nearer home in a smaller city, maybe Glasgow.'

Janice said she was pleased for him. Back out in the warm night Charlie was smiling, but that seemed to be his permanent expression.

Something must have given Charlie the idea that she would be willing to sleep with him that night, that it would be the most natural thing in the world to collapse into her bed with her – wasn't that London behaviour? But even after two pints, Janice's priorities were shifting and she put him on the lounge floor in his sleeping bag for the night. In the morning she went with him to the tube, and another rejected male crossed the black and white tiles to the trains below.

It was a relief to step out into the empty streets of Sunday morning. Janice needed to think, but something about that flat made her unable to. Instead of turning right she went in the other direction, to the park which she'd seen from the top of the bus but never visited. Why had they never once gone to their local park? It was quiet apart from churchgoers, looking spectacularly smart on their way to the Seventh Day Adventist church nearby. Janice found a bench in the sun. Sitting there, although her mind was in turmoil, she closed the door on this strange episode. She wished that these two men whom she'd once found attractive had stayed in the worlds where she'd met them and not strayed into her life now.

What was to be her new and proper world she didn't know. She was a good student, and would finish her degree next summer. For the first time in her life, she thought of studying coming to an end and the necessity of earning proper money. She needed to move out of that basement. If a friend would store her things for the summer, she could go home to Liverpool until just before the start of the autumn term and find another place to live.

With that thought, Janice returned to the flat. The bill for the rent was on the floor. She called Lavinia, who lived in a large rented house. Lavinia agreed to store her trunk, and invited her to come for dinner and stay the night. She ordered a taxi for six o'clock. That decided, she called her mum, who was delighted her daughter would be coming home for the whole summer.

She turned on Radio 1. *Good Vibrations* by the Beach Boys was playing. She loved that song, needed it now. Singing along to all the parts, Janice wrote out the last cheque for the rent and began to pack her things. The phone didn't ring.

Across the Road

Across the Road

Monday morning was 'management information'. I stared at the screen, looking at my team's performance on a number of targets. I printed out the pages and my pencil hovered ready to circle any impressive improvements. None. At last, it was midday.

In the street the sun was glancing off the dark glass of the tower opposite. I love the City – it's just a pity that you have to spend most of the day *inside* its buildings. There were groups of young men standing in shirt sleeves eating baguettes, pairs of girls sitting clutching their diet cokes as they reported on the weekend. As I turned towards the river, a crocodile of chattering school children dodged past me. Where had all *my* youthful excitement gone? Breathing the cool air on the bridge cheered me up. My expensive shoes looked good and were comfortable, worth the money.

On the South Bank, waiters wiped tables, lingering to enjoy the sun. I bought a newspaper, sat down, ordered lunch and turned to the sports pages. As my Caesar salad arrived, I looked up. Across the road, a girl emerged from a doorway. She looks like my Emily, I thought, then realised she *was* my Emily. She walked a hundred yards along the pavement and stood at the lights. I should have got up and gone to meet her but I didn't. I hid behind my newspaper. She was frowning, immersed in her own thoughts, absent-mindedly trying to rearrange her wispy blonde hair. Her favourite low-cut summer dress was now too tight for her. That old boxy shoulder bag looked really old-fashioned. She crossed over, turned towards the bridge. I let her walk away and still didn't get up.

She'd come out of a black door with a large brass plaque. She hadn't told me she was going there today. I ate and paid for my lunch and then went to read what it said – *Henry Devine Theatrical Agent.* That made sense. Emily was still holding out for acting work but nothing was happening for her. She'd studied Drama and English at Nottingham and immediately after graduating starred at the Playhouse with an eight-week run, but since then, after two years of failed auditions, she'd had to resort to English tutoring.

On the way back to the office I brooded about this negative reaction to a girl I lived with and thought I loved. How would I feel this evening when I saw her at home?

I returned to my desk, opened my emails and saw the agenda for our Team Leaders' meeting at

4.30. I really had to dredge something positive from my data.

'Would you like anything from the sandwich bar?' asked a voice.

I looked up to see the new girl smiling at me. I thanked her but said I was fine and got on with my work. She was wearing a pale blue fitted top, which perked me up quite a bit.

Later, at the meeting, although there was no really good news, I pointed out that in the present difficult financial situation it was a good thing that our figures were maintaining their level rather than going down. I didn't stay for a drink afterwards, just got home as quickly as I could.

'Emily? Where are you?'

'In the kitchen, where else?'

'OK. What's for dinner?'

'I bought some chicken livers.'

'Sounds good.' I looked carefully at her. She seemed on edge, leafing through a copy of *The Stage,* looking for acting roles.

'What did you get up to today?' I asked.

'I went to see that theatrical agent I told you about.'

'Who?'

'I told you. Remember that party we went to in Balham two weeks ago and I met an agent.'

'Oh yes.' I remembered the party but not the agent.

'At the party he seemed really positive. Took a real interest in me. Said I ought to come to his agency and have a proper chat, so I went to see him today.'

'And?'

'Turns out he's just a charming guy and the only thing he could offer me was voice overs.'

'Right. Did you take him up on it?'

Emily got up suddenly, and wrenched a bag of frozen spinach out of the freezer. 'No, David, I didn't. You know perfectly well what I'm looking for.'

'Yes, but will you ever find it? You might *enjoy* doing voice overs for the time being.'

'My friend Jan did them – it sounded just dreadful, depressing and not well-paid.'

'But you're scarcely earning *anything* at the moment.' We were slipping into the usual argument about her work. Could be dangerous.

'Maybe you'd like me to work at *McDonald's?*'

'That's silly, but I can't see why you don't brainstorm the whole thing, be systematic about it, write yourself an action plan.'

Shaking her head in disbelief, she tore the top off a packet of something and emptied it into a saucepan. 'You and your business techniques – you don't understand that creative people don't operate like that. We target specific opportunities.'

'Which you keep missing.'

'That's a horrible thing to say. I'm here backing you up, shopping, making dinners, cleaning the flat, planning our social life. If you were the one out of work, I don't think I'd be getting quite the same service.'

'This is not the point. What matters is that you get out of the house and do something reasonably suited to your talents.'

'I'm not earning very much but I'm doing my best. It's OK for you. You've got a job. But are *you* happy in it? You seem to spend most of your time complaining about what you do. How did you get on today for example?'

'Fine,' I lied.

Across from me at the table, Emily's hair was falling into the rice and her baggy T shirt had a stain on it. 'Emily, can I say something?'

'You can say what you like.'

'It's your appearance – you're not taking care of yourself as well as you used to. If you're aiming to be on the stage, you'll need to dress a bit more cutting edge.'

Emily looked up at me, speechless. She put down her fork, got up, wiped her hands on her jeans, fetched her jacket and handbag and walked out of the flat, slamming the door.

Well, at least I had faced up to it, said what I thought. She didn't have to react like that. I was even going to suggest a day out to treat her to some new clothes and a haircut. She'd be back. Just needed a walk around the block to cool off, like my mother used to.

My mobile rang. It was my friend Joe. He was staying overnight in town, and did I want to join him for a drink? I jumped at the chance. It had been a bad day, couldn't get worse. He agreed to meet me in our local in about half an hour. I had a shower and changed.

As I went in he waved me over. It was always good to see Joe. We had a couple of beers. I said that Emily was out but not that she'd *walked* out and painted a fairly respectable picture of our lives. Joe's news was that he had broken up with his girlfriend and was having a bit of difficulty with internet dating.

On the way home I wondered if Emily would be there or if she'd go off to stay with a friend. She'd never walked out before. There was silence in the flat. The bedroom door was closed. The remains of the meal and dirty dishes had been left, so I cleaned up. Emily didn't emerge from the bedroom. It was late when I joined her.

She was curled up with her back to me and didn't turn round. I looked down at her before lying down and saw that her face was wet with tears. I climbed in behind her, slid my arms around her waist and clasped her tight.

Red Bikini

Red Bikini

They've been on the beach fifteen minutes without saying anything. Half term tiredness has finally kicked in. Becky fishes in her bag for her mobile and takes a photo of the curve of the bay, the Sunday sunbathers and the castle on the headland. She wonders how the name *Tossa de Mar* relates to the castle – is it an old word for *turrets*? She takes out her guide book and finds this to be correct. She wonders if holiday photos could be used for her language-teaching. 'How can the sea be so calm after that terrible storm last night?' she says aloud, turning to Clare.

No answer. Eyes shut, Clare is stretched out on the sunbed, sunglasses on, earphones in, probably lost in a Beethoven sonata, her pale skin reddening under the suntan oil. A beach rug unfolded nearby releases a whiff of ancient perfume. A little girl practises her ballet steps under a parasol, watched by her proud grandma on a fold-up chair.

A new couple walk down the beach and claim an empty patch. So casual, just a towel each. They peel off shorts and T shirts and sit down facing the sea. She's wearing a red bikini. Short fair hair, biscuit-coloured skin like his but his hair is dark. She looks healthy, a bit younger than him, but their bodies are both compact, in good shape. She's got her head down, engrossed in something already, but he's restless.

Clare sits up, removes the ear-phones, pushes her long hair back. 'What are you looking at?' she asks.

'That couple.'

'Great bikini.' Clare says. 'It's not red and not orange, somewhere in between.'

He has now joined in with her activity, heads bent together. Becky thinks it's a crossword. 'And look how well they get on,' she says. 'Made for each other, wouldn't you say? Wonder how long they've been married.'

Clare opens her novel, says nothing. Becky continues to watch. The woman gets up. Hands on hips, she looks out to sea. She's wondering whether to go in or not. Leaning on his elbow he stays with the crossword for a moment then stands up too. She turns to him, smiles, comes near but not touching, moves the sand about with her toe, points out something across the bay, gently straightens out the waistband of his swim-shorts for him. They go down to the sea, stand there a while ankle deep, then, arms out for balance, she goes in up to her waist. He follows and they plunge in together.

'They're not married,' says Clare, looking up from her book.

Becky hears but doesn't respond. They're not in the sea for long. Becky has noticed before how the Spanish behave differently from the Brits. This is just a normal Sunday morning for them, off-season, summer tourists gone from their beach. At the water's edge they stand talking in groups. The beach is just where they happen to be. Nobody's building sand-castles or running wildly into the waves.

The couple come back up the beach and stand in the sun to dry off. Now it's his turn to make the moves. He puts one hand on her right buttock and takes it off again. He moves closer so their shoulders are touching, tries to make her laugh, but for some reason she's not reacting.

'What makes you assume they're not married?' Becky asks Clare.

'They're having an affair.'

'How do you know?'

'Because I'm having one myself.'

Becky takes a moment or two to react to Clare's sudden revelation. The two had bonded when they both took up their first teaching job three years before. Clare was shy and glad to have someone to share the horrors of the first months in the classroom. Now settled in their different departments, they're no longer so close, but Becky remembers Clare telling her on one of the Foreign Languages school trips to France that she had never really found anyone to be a proper boyfriend and what comforted her most was music.

'Wow, you kept *that* quiet. So who is he?'

'Patrick. He's a musician.'

'What's he like?'

'Tall, curly hair, cuddly, affectionate.'

'And he's married?'

'Yes. They came over from Ireland married.

Becky's thoughts go straight to her husband Robert, hard at work in his office at this very moment. They've been married five years now. Just imagine if it was time for him to be tempted by all these younger women moving around him all day long. 'And do you think he's going to leave her to be with you?' she asks.

'Easy does it, Becky. I've only known him a year. He conducts our choir.'

'How do you manage to see each other?'

'Every Wednesday after choir. He tells his wife we all go for a drink.'

'Does he love you?'

'He's never said, but I love him. I adore him.'

Clare watches a pair of women arrive and settle near the rocky end of the bay. They look alike, sisters probably, or close friends. They're free of beach-bags, children, sunshades, just themselves. One has a bottle green swimsuit with white baroque swirls and the other's is black and red. Sturdy but good figures, probably in their forties. Perhaps they have their freedom today for too short or too long a time. Their husbands or mothers have maybe consented to being left with the children while the Sunday lunch cooks or could they all be meeting up later to eat out? Now they're standing facing each other, changing position every so often trying to show they are still attractive, heads nodding and shaking as if engaged in a serious topic.

'Clare, you're going to have a job on your hands if you're trying to make him leave his wife for you.'

'I'm not *trying* to do that, Becky.'

'OK, *hoping* then. Don't you miss him all the time?'

'I love seeing him, but I'm also used to being on my own and I'm good at it. This is the first time in my life I've ever known what it's like to be with a man and I'm really happy.'

Becky looks over towards the lovely couple but they've gone. Back to their room? Their weekend nearly over? Do they work together? Are they work colleagues, here under cover of a conference?

Clare has more to say. 'It has its ups and downs. I can't say I don't wonder sometimes how it'll turn out. And if he says Gail and he are growing apart, I'll dare to hope, then he'll tell me something routine they've done together and I feel rubbish.'

An old man approaches, a folded canvas seat in one hand and a thick paperback in the other. He puts the book on the sand while setting up his chair, shakily sits down on it, rescues the book and begins to read. He's wedged in, narrowly confined, and doesn't want to look around.

'A Brit,' whispers Becky to Clare.

'Poor old thing,' she whispers back. 'It's not good to be on your own when you're old.'

From behind, there's a sudden rush of traffic noise. They stand and look up at the high balustrade. A ribbon of Volkswagen Beetles has been sneaking its way quietly around the bay and is beginning to creep up the steep hill towards the next inlet of this rugged coast – all colours, all models, a big European family of proud cars, their horns start sounding in their different notes and volumes, not aggressively, just in solidarity. The man in the chair has got up too. There's a grey-haired woman in a white blouse waving down at him. He sees her immediately and becomes suddenly so alive and happy, it's as if he'd thought he might never see her again. Perhaps she doesn't like beaches, or was once a Beetle owner herself.

'It's all going on in Tossa today,' says Clare. 'I'm getting hungry, what about you?'

'Yes. We could try and find a place to eat or just go out for dinner in the evening and get chips for now. There's a stand over there.'

'Good plan, Becky. Remember those chips in Calais?'

'The best chips in the world, on the quai, just before getting back on the boat, oily *frites*, with mayo.'

As they sit on the little wall removing the sand from between their toes, Clare says, 'Have you noticed, we haven't talked about school at all, not for a moment?'

'Isn't it great? Let's not,' says Becky.

The chips are a bit dry, with only ketchup. A little tourist train appears with cream painted cars. Its fat rubber tyres squeak as it rounds the bend towards its stop.

'Come on. Let's catch it,' says Clare. Out of breath, they pile on to a hard wooden seat and wait for the train to fill up. Becky takes a photo of the busy terrace of an ice-cream parlour on the other side of the promenade and sends it to Robert with a quick text. 'Clare,' she says, 'look who's over there.' The Red Bikini couple sit calmly looking out to sea eating their ice-creams.

Becky looks at Clare and they laugh. 'I tell you what we'll do tonight,' she says, 'we'll go and get a *sangria* before dinner.'

'Perfect,' says Clare.

Becky fast-forwards their little holiday in her mind – two whole days left and then fly home. That's why Clare chose to be home by Wednesday –

in time for choir and Patrick. Anyway, she herself feels glad to have a couple of days to prepare lessons before the weekend. Robert will pick them up at the airport. He might even make a dinner, and they'll plan a nice weekend. She'll buy him a present from Tossa.

The train jerks and moves off to take them through the narrow streets of the Old Town.

Girl in a Hurry

Girl in a Hurry

Joe and I hadn't been living in the country for long before we got into the habit of going to dances in the village hall, organised by the primary school or the playing field. This sort of thing didn't go on in London. One hot Saturday evening in June, we'd been dancing to the Rolling Stones. We loved the fast dances but joined the crowd leaving the floor when it came to the slow medley. That night only a few couples were left, stranded in their intimacy, happy enough in themselves to be watched by us all sitting at our tables.

Right in the centre of the floor, a young couple began dancing but quickly came to a standstill, involved in a passionate kiss, their eyes shut, she guiding his head down with a fistful of his woolly blonde hair. Short and slender, and engulfed completely by his taller and more ample body, she could not have been more than 20 while he was nearer 30. We all noticed, our heads drawn together sharing knowledge or straining to overhear what was being said around us. Even the other dancing couples stole more than a passing glance. As the last bars of the ballad trailed away, she was on tip-toe with her arms around his neck. He scooped up her small light frame, lowered her gently to the floor and she, taking his hand, led him out through the double doors. The entertainment was over but not the story.

Joe liked a scandal. He was listening to gossip from the next table.

'That's Tom Anderson,' someone said, 'but *she's* not his wife.'

'No. She's new, isn't she?' asked someone else. 'Doesn't she live in the council houses?'

There were so many new arrivals in the village at that time that even the locals found it hard to keep up. The residents of Upper Green, where the council houses were, and those of Lower Green, the older part, were separate populations who knew of, but didn't socialize with, each other. As for us, we hardly knew anybody's name, even in Upper Green where we lived.

I had seen the man around, walking to the shop, coming out of the pub, and once looking very out of place at the school gate. What struck me most about him was a resigned expression too old for his age. He lumbered along, hands in the pockets of his long black leather jacket, shoulders drooping, his long face hiding shyly behind bushy hair. The child-like slip of a girl I hadn't seen before.

I found out more the week after the dance. At

the school gate, I'd got to know Caroline, whose children had befriended ours when they first arrived, and one day after school we went round to her house. The children were immediately busy in the garden with dogs, cats and small animals in cages, while I waited inside for the tea. There was nothing smart about the room – it felt as if outside was where everything happened and indoors was just a place where you sheltered from really bad weather. I wondered about Caroline's husband. He didn't have a job but never seemed to be at home.

After a few minutes, when I brought up the dance-floor incident, Caroline began to explain.

'She's the wife of Steve Taylor. They moved in next door to the Andersons about two months ago, and she's already gone off with Tom.' Then she put her mug down on the table, folded her arms and looked near to tears. 'I can't understand what made her do it. Lisa Anderson's my friend. They're a lovely family – three little girls not even school age. Steve Taylor is also a nice chap. Lisa said they'd been good neighbours up to now, having barbecues together every night in this hot spell.'

'And do the Taylors have children too?' I asked.

'Twin boys, just started school.'

'So, where are they all living now?'

Caroline ignored my question, started to cry.

'Why did Tom fall for her, for goodness' sake? She's not even that good looking. I don't know what's happening these days. She's torn apart a happy family. For what?'

'I'm sorry,' I said. I didn't mean to upset you.'

She dried her eyes with the back of her hand, propped herself up with a cushion, took a breath. 'It's all right,' she said, resigned. 'Tom Anderson and the girl have managed to get to stay in his place with two of his three girls. Lisa has taken just the oldest one back to her mother's in the next village. Steve Taylor and his twins have moved to a rented cottage along the main road. He's had to sell his car and give up his job to look after them.' Caroline regarded 'the new woman' with such suspicion and resentment that she never used her name, which is why to this day I don't know it.

'What a mess.' I said.

'Saturday night would be the first time they were out together,' Caroline finished, getting up. It was time to go.

I drove home with my two children in the back seat, mulling over the fall-out from this double break-up and realising for the first time how stable our family was. During the last weeks of that school term, I thought about it a lot. Affairs went on in this village as they had in London. Families split up. Messy at the time, but heading for something better? And to make something new, you had to break down what you had to start with. You met someone right and special too late when everything was settled around you. Would you dare to go for it?

Steve Taylor appeared for the first time at the school gate. He was the one leaping after the twins who always ran off. His desperate commands were ignored as he chased after them down the road. He had no car and it was a long walk for young children there and back. I pictured him in his lonely cottage, giving them their tea, getting them ready for bed, entertaining them all day by himself during the weekends, shopping, cleaning up. I hoped their mother would have time to come and see them, but how could they even be on speaking terms?

Then I thought of Lisa Anderson at her mother's in the next village, on the sofa watching T.V. cuddled up to her one little girl, not wanting to put her to bed. I imagined Tom Anderson's new household with the other two girls upstairs already fast asleep, and 'the new woman' with their dad downstairs. Why did I think they would be perfectly all right in spite of missing their mother? Perhaps because this new woman had such conviction about the rightness of what she was doing. While they were kissing on the dance floor I'd noticed the urgency of her movements, her determination to push this through, her disregard for the watching villagers. It was as if she were establishing their couple status once and for all so there could be no doubt. They'd both come to the dance in jeans and T-shirts, having not had time to dress up like the rest of us.

For the rest of the year, the new Anderson family seemed invisible, but the following summer, we were all up at the playing field for the school sports. There was a mothers' race. There were cheers as good-hearted, unfit and out-of breath mums charged along on the grass when a slender athletic figure overtook them, cruising without effort to the tape. It was her. The cheering died away.

'Who's she?' a woman behind me asked.

'It's that girl, her that ran off with Tom Anderson,' was the reply.

Five years passed. Both our children travelled to secondary education on the school bus so I lost contact with the friends I'd made at the village school. Caroline split up with her husband and moved away. I went back to work in the nearest town, 45 minutes away by car, and we attended only a few village events.

Then, one Saturday morning, I was waiting in the car outside the village shop for Joe to buy a newspaper, when I saw her. She jumped down out of an old Land Rover and vanished into the shop. Tom Anderson was in the driving seat, completely transformed. He was slim with a short haircut. Looking relaxed and confident, he turned to the back to supervise a dog and some children. I couldn't see how many. As she came out with her shopping, I saw her up close for the first time – a pale face with freckles on a small upturned nose, hair light in colour and texture, still wearing T-shirt and jeans. She moved economically, like a dancer, head high, looking forward, not noticing anyone else. She opened the door, threw the bag on the floor and flew up beside it, strapping herself in and smoothing her hair, and they were off.

I was so busy watching that Joe startled me as he got back into the car and slammed the door.

'You'll never guess who was in that Land-Rover,' I said.

'Who?' he said, feigning interest.

I told him. 'I think they've had children of their own,' I said, ready to speculate further, but Joe's thoughts had already shifted elsewhere as we pulled away.

I felt so relieved and happy for them that the whole story went out of my mind for several years. It was on the day I went to see Fran Baxter on Upper Green that I found myself thinking about her again. We were planning a party and Joe wanted quite a lot of beer. Fran worked at the brewery and was going to help me look at prices and put in an order. We used to do this for events we ran while on the school committee together. I decided on some Belgian lager and we filled in the form. On the door-step on my way out I brought up the topic casually as if it were of no importance.

'Fran,' I said, 'You remember when Mr Anderson split up with his wife that time and there was that girl – do you know if they're still together?'

Fran's low tolerance of infidelity and preference for locals over in-movers, made this a difficult topic, but she delivered the news with delicacy.

'Oh!' she said. 'Didn't you know? She had cancer. She died. I'd say about three years ago.'

The phone rang and Fran went back inside to answer it. I caught her eye and waved myself off. I had no right to be horrified by this knowledge as I hadn't even known the girl and so much time had passed, but I was. I got into the car and drove around instead of going home. How long had she known she was ill? She'd snatched her chance of happiness, built up a new world for herself with Tom Anderson and his children, and maybe now children of their own, but they'd had such a short time together – less than ten years. I couldn't bear to think of him trying to manage without her now.

Finally, a few months after hearing about her death, on a sunny September morning, I was driving out of the village in the opposite direction from usual, when I noticed a young girl emerging from the Anderson house. Neatly dressed in the high school summer uniform, she waited calmly on the pavement as I drove past, and suddenly I knew who she must be. I imagined her being capable and a comfort to her father and the younger children. With her woolly hair and upturned nose, she looked as if all was right with the world as she crossed the road to catch the school bus.

Two Girls

Two Girls

'Josh! Come in,' says Paul. 'Welcome to Hackney.'

'Paul, you're the best. So happy to be here. Thanks for having me.'

'No trouble. That's your room. Put your bag in and come and talk to me. Cup of tea?'

'I'd love one, thanks.'

'You look a bit hot.'

'Just a bit. I walked around Paddington all morning, then the Tube was packed and we were held up in the tunnel for a bit, but it was all great. I love being here.'

'You know, I haven't seen you since our flat in Camden Town.'

'Remember it well. Your kitchen here is just like ours, except that it's a lot tidier and cleaner!'

We take the tea into a small lounge. He's got two enormous old armchairs, a TV, and a table stacked with folders and books.

'Is that your school work, Paul?'

'It is. But don't let's look at it. It's Friday night, and Half Term! I want to hear exactly what *you've* been up to these last two years.'

'I've been sharing a flat in Reading, doing an admin job I got through an agency. It pays quite well but I can't see it leading to anything. As a town, Reading is OK, but feels too much like being back home. Studying in London made me feel so wonderful. There's nowhere like it.'

'I suppose I take London for granted as I'm from here, but while I'm at work I'm confined to one little district.'

'How do you like teaching?' I ask him.

'It's hard, but it gets better. These kids – we can help them such a lot, and most want to be helped.'

Paul takes his buzzing mobile out of his pocket, reads a text and types a response. 'That was Julia. We're going to meet her at the other end of London Fields in about an hour.'

'Is she a teacher too?' I ask.

'No,' says Paul. 'She works in the City – a real high flier.'

The air smells of smoke and marinade. On the grass either side of the path, groups stand turning burgers and drinking out of plastic glasses. Children run around in circles; bikers whiz past. 'The Council provides this barbecue area in the summer,' Paul says. 'I used to go last year with friends, but Julia isn't into that kind of thing.'

Julia's already at the gate, posed like a

cardboard cut-out in front of the pedestrian street opposite, thronged with young people. She's wearing a crisp cotton sun dress with yellow and white stripes. It's slightly pear shaped and just skirts the knees, so that with her neat short hair, she's fully contained within her outline. Slim, tanned, lovely, she beams at me and shakes my hand. This feels like my first interview.

We follow her across the road. She dodges her way through the tall young men in shorts and T shirts standing on the cobbles, dangling their bottles of beer. The grey brick façades of the 19th century terraced houses shrink back from this modern crowd squealing and laughing. Waiters hop on and off the kerb serving those savvy enough to be already settled at the small tables on the narrow pavement. Greek, Turkish, Italian, anything you want – steaks, kebabs, fried fish. I'm really hungry, but we're to get drinks first. Julia guides us towards high tables outside a pub where you can stand, and bags the very last empty one.

Paul goes inside to get the drinks. I glance at Julia but her eyes are scanning as if looking for something or someone. They steady for a moment. She seems relieved, turns her head in my direction.

'That's a lovely dress, Julia,' I say. 'Perfect for a night like this.'

'Thanks. My mum made it. She's always made my dresses. I'm an only child and she's still trying to do everything for me.'

'Paul told me you work in the City, but not exactly what you do.'

'I work for a big bank, look after the accounts of our wealthiest customers. I like the work but it's a very male environment at my level. I'm the only woman. And what about you? Paul felt you needed a challenge. What sort of work are you looking for?'

'I've got a degree in English, so it's not obvious!'

'Have you thought of copywriting? I've got a friend who works in an advertising agency. I can give you his details if you like.'

I was right. This *is* my first interview. I hear myself accept her kind offer but feel out of my depth. It's time I did some serious thinking.

'Cheers!' says Paul returning with the drinks. 'Sun, friends, half-term ahead. What more do we want?'

Julia takes two gulps of her cold Chardonnay then excuses herself.

'Where's she off to?' I ask Paul.

'We came here last Friday night and Julia got involved with that girl over there. Spent ages talking to her.'

A few yards away, leaning against the wall of a closed down boutique, a girl sits by herself on the pavement, beer bottle at her side, rolling up a cigarette. No one is talking to her and she's not part of the crowd. We watch as Julia reaches her and stops, hands on hips. The girl peers up from under her messy hair, squinting in the sun. She stops fumbling with her half-made roll-up, and, pushing her hair back from her forehead, tries to take in what Julia's saying. Her face is red and blotchy. She pulls up her long skirt to show wounds on her legs, covers them up again and clutches herself like a child. Suddenly Julia is crouching down beside her, but then the girl draws back as Julia seems to threaten her. She's holding a ten pound note right up against the girl's nose. We can't hear what she's saying. Julia pulls her hand away as if teasing a child, crams the note back in her pocket and stands up. Brushing herself down, she turns and walks back to us.

'I told her,' she hisses, shaking with anger, 'I *told* her. I gave her money last week on condition she went to get help. Well, she didn't. Made all sorts of excuses. Did she think I would keep on giving her money like that?'

'Help with what?' I ask.

'Rehab,' says Paul.

I look back towards the girl, but the shop front area is empty. Julia has gone too, in the other direction, pushing her way through the crowd. Paul is following her. Keeping them in sight, I walk behind. Paul puts his arm around her shoulders as she stumbles along in tears. I want to leave them in peace, so I run up and tell Paul there's something I'd like to look at along the road and I'll be back at the flat in half an hour.

This street's name is Broadway. It's far too narrow for what's going on in it at the moment, but gradually the crowds at the popular end thin out to just a few people sipping wine outside a quieter pub. A florist is bringing in jugs of orange orchids. She must be closing. I ask her if I can still buy something. She says it's OK and to take my time. I choose a bunch of anemones, which costs twice as much as I'm expecting. There's no sign of the girl. Walking back, twice as hungry as before, I see diners on the terrace fork up their Bolognese. I begin to picture myself settled here, doing a proper job, having a girlfriend, coming here on a Friday night. How could I have stayed away for so long? I need to live here.

I ring the bell. Paul is on his own.

'What happened?' I ask.

'Oh, it's OK,' he says. 'She'll be all right. Gone back home to change. She didn't like what she was wearing.'

'But she was really upset.'

'Yeah, she was. I tried to tell her last week to leave the girl alone but she was determined to see what she could do.' He pours us a beer. 'We had a big argument about it.'

Paul looks as if he doesn't want to talk about this any more, so I change the subject and ask him about the flat. Is he renting or buying it?

Spluttering into his beer, he laughs. 'Renting. The price of a tiny flat around here is £600,000. A whole house is over a million.'

I nod, feeling out of touch and naïve.

'Don't worry,' he says. 'If you want to move to London, you'll work it out. You were always good at that.'

Julia arrives back, in a short floppy dress with a jeans jacket. She looks out at us from under puffy eyelids. 'I'm sorry,' she says.

Paul takes her in his arms. 'Come on, let's go. I've booked us for 8.30 at the Indian restaurant, the quiet one.'

I hold out the anemones for her.

Outside, there's a soft screen of rain falling. Julia links arms with both of us. And in the restaurant, she says, 'Let's not say any more about what happened earlier. I'll just tell you this: last Friday, when I went over to her, she looked up at me with a smile which said, '*you're my best friend.*'

Do Well, Go Far

Do Well, Go Far

'I'll get the drinks,' said Rob, standing up. This was kind of him as it was the first time he'd come to one of these gatherings. He took their orders. Danielle watched the tall awkward figure of her old boyfriend edge through the jostling backs to the bar, where shots were lined up for a crowd of laughing girls.

Looking around the circle of her old A level class, those who'd stayed at home rather than going away to university, she sensed a definite trend of pairing up, settling down. Now in their mid-twenties, some were still together after meeting in Sixth Form, others were with new boyfriends or girlfriends. Danielle's current flatmate, Gemma, looked particularly radiant beside Stan, her man of the moment.

When Rob returned with the drinks, and sat back down beside her, there was a surprise announcement from Gemma – she and Stan had got engaged. Danielle raised her glass with everybody else in an outburst of congratulations and real excitement from the girls admiring the ring and asking about the wedding. Then it dawned on her that Rob, who hadn't ever been part of these Saturday night gatherings, had been invited by Gemma. Why? Well, of course, on the off-chance there might be a re-match between Rob and herself. Annoyed at the interference and uncomfortable about being one of the few in the group still on her own, she swallowed her pride – Gemma had meant well. She turned to Rob. He hadn't wanted to break up at the time, but was probably over it by now. In any case, he was good to talk to.

He said he had a job in a call-centre for an insurance company which was quite well paid and he might soon be promoted to Team Leader. He hadn't gone to uni because his family couldn't afford it. He asked Danielle about her job.

'I'm an admin assistant in the Biology Department at London University,' she said. 'I can do it easily. I get annoyed with the students though. You should hear the idiotic questions they ask at our Queries window. And every time I collect up exam papers, I feel I should be one of them and not an office worker.'

'Why didn't you go off to uni? You were thinking about Edinburgh, weren't you?'

'I was, but in the end, Mum, being on her own, just didn't want me to go away.'

'But you could have applied somewhere in London with your good grades.'

'I know, but guess what, Mum's friend was a secretary in another Department there and got me the job where I am now. Just as good, she assured me.'

Danielle heard herself being miserable and didn't like it. Rob was making the best of his situation and all she could do was complain.

Next day was the weekly visit home to Mill Hill. Nothing ever changed in that house. Did Mum want things to stay exactly the same as when Dad had died 13 years ago? Couldn't she go out to work? There was no need because of Dad's pension. She'd left employment for good after they got married. It was hard to bring up any of this.

The table was set. Mum brought in the roast lamb. It was her chance to catch up with Danielle's week. 'How did the pub go last night?' she asked.

'Gemma and Stan have got engaged.'

'Oh, how lovely,' she said, and then, with mock indifference, 'and I believe Rob was there.'

'Yes, he was there.'

Mum was waiting for more.

'Mum, you know that's over. We had a good chat though.'

'You used to get on well, and you always looked right together, both so tall and slim. Such a nice boy.' Mum dabbed her napkin at her mouth and ran her fingers across the lace cloth. She wasn't going to cry, was she?

Danielle asked about her week. A trip into town with her friend Jean, cards on Wednesday night, and Sue across the road had just become a grandmother.

At two o'clock, before she left, Danielle put her arms around her mother as usual, and noticed over her shoulder, that something *was* different – the globe was missing from its table in the corner, replaced by a vase of artificial flowers.

'Mum, where's my globe?'

'That old thing. I gave it in to the charity shop.'

'Dad bought me that. He taught me the countries. He taught me the capital cities – I used to spin it round.'

'It was falling to bits. I'll get you another one for your birthday if you like.'

Danielle shut the gate and walked towards the Tube. Her Dad had meant the world to her. He'd used that globe to teach her almost everything she knew, big important things, like that it was hottest at the equator because it was nearer the sun. He showed her where he'd been during his Navy years. She remembered him sitting patiently helping her with Maths homework. He was the one who always told her she was a clever girl, that she would do well and go far. When he left the Navy, without much education, he'd worked his way up to a very good job in the Royal Mail. She *was* clever, had got three As at A level, but now was not doing well and had gone nowhere at all.

At the Tube station, the kiosk was still open so she bought her favourite glossy magazine to read in the train, but was unable to concentrate. Saturday nights in the pub with the Sixth Form crowd or out with a friend, working nine to five in a dull job, going to see her mum every Sunday – that was really all her life consisted of. Even turning the fashion pages failed to inspire her this time. She looked around at her fellow passengers, envying the younger women who always seemed to be wearing something new. She didn't buy much these days. Sitting in an office all day had made her bulge in the wrong places.

She went on to the features section. Her dismal thoughts prevailed until a title caught her eye, *How to Make Yourself More Attractive to Men*.

The secret is not outward appearance, it read, *but inner confidence. Men are attracted to happy women who are sure of themselves. Research has shown that it is often through extreme personal challenge that true self-confidence is acquired.*

The list of challenges suggested was laughable – keeping goats, going camping with a person you didn't get on with, eating foods you detest for a week. It must be time to give up glossy magazines, she thought, when the final challenge made her sit up – *go on a foreign holiday by yourself.*

It was Archway station. Danielle bundled the magazine into her bag and got off the train. Now this really had made her think. Turning into her street she thought of a distant holiday, but by the time she reached her door she'd persuaded herself it would be more fun to go with a girlfriend.

Gemma was out, staying at Stan's. Danielle went online. Many possibilities, but December was the cheapest month. Having worked since she was 18, she'd saved quite a bit and there actually were a few destinations warm enough at that time.

She phoned her friend Lindsay. No good. Her

holiday was already booked. Curled up on the sofa to finish the article, she read, *Decide what sort of holiday you want.* She'd only been abroad once, for a week with Rob, and he'd organised everything. She got out a pad and pencil to jot down some ideas, which took quite a while. Just before midnight a great deal was crossed out but Danielle was sure about *luxury, quiet* and *top-class beach.*

Final tip: *Book at least six months in advance to give you time to lose weight and buy new outfits to look your best.*

This idea was becoming realistic, but how scary would it be? Feeling lonely in a strange place with a foreign language, knowing no one. Then her eye caught the photos of sea and sky. Surely it would be great to be in *any* of these beautiful places even without a friend? *NOW BOOK THAT HOLIDAY,* it finished.

'I will! I will!' she said aloud.

The next weekend, she booked a late December beach holiday in a four-star hotel in a quiet resort where the temperature would be 70 degrees. By mid-May, she'd lost three pounds thanks to a diet from the same magazine and was doing a work-out twice a week at a gym. She went down two clothes sizes. In August her summer outfits came from the sales. All through this preparation she didn't tell anyone she was going on holiday by herself. In the office they all thought she was going with a girlfriend. The week before, she called her mum and broke the news, which didn't go down well, but that was too bad.

In early December her colleagues were occupied with the usual Christmas count-down, how behind they all were with their Christmas shopping, how Oxford Street was already so busy you could hardly move. For once, Danielle said nothing, having already bought and wrapped her few presents. She'd be back by the 23rd. Anyway, thoughts of her beautiful holiday had lifted her right out of the tinsel tangle.

On the 16th December, all ready to leave, she went over to her dad's photo in its silver-frame. His mouth was closed in a smile and he looked out at her kindly in a dreamy, tired sort of way. She wondered if he was already ill when the photo was taken. 'Wish me luck, Dad,' she said, then, changing her mind, told him he was coming with her and zipped him into the case.

Danielle kept herself busy reading her novel and the flight passed quickly. The plane curved and swooped over a wide bay on a kidney shaped island, whizzed down above the sandy landscape and bumped on to the runway. There was a roaring of brakes, clicking of seat belts and the door was opened.

The air was warm and perfumed with unknown plants. She walked along a wide corridor lined with bright advertisements in Spanish into a huge almost empty arrivals hall, newly built, she thought, still with a scent of fresh plaster.

The coach stopped at several hotels. It was strange that only a few Brits got out at hers, which seemed the best one. Through large windows, the afternoon sun glinted over a cream marble-floored foyer where chains of silver lights, banks of scarlet poinsettia and a tall narrow tree hung with oversized golden balls blended Christmas into this 'summer' paradise.

A porter showed her to her room. Catching sight of herself in the mirror she was surprised to see that she was not an ugly contrast with these surroundings but actually looked as if she belonged; but as the door closed behind the smiling Spanish face, Danielle felt a first shiver of isolation. She went straight out on to the balcony. Looking down on a stream of cars and vans driving along the main road going about their normal business made her feel OK again. She changed into summer clothes and went out to explore before dinner.

There was a tubular lift which she called to go down. Inside was a group of older people, tanned, elegantly dressed, who nodded to her, carried on with their conversation in German, then got out, heading to the first sitting for dinner. Down on the promenade, couples were strolling on the sand in the early evening sun. The atmosphere was calm, unlike her previous holiday with Rob in a cheap noisy resort with crowded bars and small stony beaches. So this is what *four star* meant. On the left were bushes heavy with purple flowers and to the right, the wide sandy beach.

Back in the hotel, she walked along outdoor passageways painted the colour of sand and planted with palms here and there, waving in the light breeze. She looked up and saw little green fruits the size of grapes. These must be dates. How could this be the first time since A level Biology that she'd had a single thought about fruit growing on a tree? She was working in a Biology Department but entirely excluded from what the students were learning.

Inside her room she discovered she had a lounge area as part of the bedroom and a perfectly designed spacious bathroom. The room was uncluttered and every item was fit for purpose. Just as she was splashing about in her oval bath feeling nothing could go wrong, her worst fear crept up and stated itself – at dinner, you'll have to sit all by yourself at a little table and everyone will be looking at you and feeling sorry for you. Shaking with terror all the way through getting dressed, she tried to smile at herself in the mirror and rehearsed her little story about how her friend had let her down at the last minute.

Outside the large glass door to the restaurant, she felt as if she were gate-crashing a banquet – colourful arrays of luscious food, chefs serving under bright copper lights, people moving about confidently to select what they wanted. A member of the front of house staff approached, smart in his cream jacket, asked for her room number and guided her to a small table. A jovial old wine-waiter said 'Guten Abend!', drew up an ice-bucket and gave her the drinks menu from which she ordered a bottle of white wine. She spread her hands on the smooth linen cloth and smiled at the couples to her left and right, but they were German and so she wouldn't even be able to present her excuse about the friend letting her down.

She shook off her fear by getting up to explore the night's dishes. The excellence of the eating experience absorbed her for most of the evening, even though she felt people's eyes were on her all the time. Eating by yourself in London was easier – you could take a book to read – but here that would have made you even more conspicuous. She missed having a friend to talk to. There was only one young couple, and they were laughing and enjoying themselves. When she couldn't eat any more, she left the restaurant and was grateful that at least the manager said good-night to her.

On the second day, she woke up late and almost missed breakfast. The sky was overcast. She decided to spend the morning at the pool but no one was swimming. In a secluded spot with her magazine, waiting for the sun to come out, she observed from a safe vantage point the animated conversations of the Germans with their permanent tans. They all seemed to know one another. The sun did not come out. Her white tummy would give her away as not being used to this kind of holiday, but that was nothing to be ashamed of now that she was perfectly slim and would be tanned by the end of the week.

That evening, instead of the older waiter, Danielle was looked after by a tall fair young man in a white jacket.

'You speak good English,' she said.

'Thank you,' he said. 'I've worked in England. I'm from Poland.'

'Oh, really? What sort of work did you do?'

'Boring jobs at first – picking asparagus, washing cars. When I returned for a second time I got a job as a waiter in a restaurant.'

'Ah, and that's why you're here now.'

'Yes. They were looking for waiters with some English as well as German.'

Working her way through a magnificent plate of cold starters, a steak with thyme butter and a number of different desserts while sipping her white wine, she felt flattered that her waiter had spent more time talking to her than to anyone else. Now relaxed enough to observe the older couples, she noticed that many of them had nothing to say to each other and relied on the old Spanish waiters for their evening's entertainment.

The sun shone for the rest of the holiday, allowing Danielle to swim in the sea, regularly sunbathe on the beach and send some postcards. Walking along the promenade, she collected a few exotic plant-cuttings, to show her colleagues in the office. Every evening at dinner she would tell her Polish waiter all about what she'd done during the day.

Her loneliness had gone, replaced by a new sense of well-being and freedom. When she had asked for *quiet* on this holiday, she'd got it. Being with a majority of older people was restful. She often went to Reception with questions, because the staff spoke good English and were always friendly.

On the last evening, Danielle looked in the mirror before going down to dinner. The Spanish hairdresser in the hotel had styled her dark hair into a simpler shorter cut which enhanced the shape of her face and got rid of her usual tousled look. Creamy silver eye-shadow and black mascara had made her brown eyes sparkle. Her arms and legs were now a shimmering reddish brown, smoothed by body-lotion and shown off by her sleeveless shift dress in several shades of green and blue.

Weaving her way through the tables, she saw

she was attracting admiring glances. People looked up and smiled at her. She became more open to them too, and realised that the German couples on either side were willing and able to speak in English about their travels in the UK. She enjoyed every mouthful of her last dinner and the Polish waiter brought her a final glass of wine.

'I never asked you your name,' she said.

'It's on my badge,' he said, pointing. 'It's Marek. What's yours?'

'Oh, so it is. I'm sorry. Mine's Danielle.'

'And so, Danielle, how have you enjoyed your holiday?'

'It's been the best. I don't want to go home. Imagine all that cold and snow. What about you, do you get to go home for Christmas?'

'Yes, I do. I'm going home to Poland for a week. More cold and snow!'

They laughed. Marek seemed pleased to talk to her.

'Do you enjoy it here?' she asked. 'Will you carry on?'

'I've got used to it, but it's a bit lonely. Most of the staff are Spanish. They trained here and stayed on. The guests are pleasant but I don't have much contact with them. Usually they will hand me a tip on their last day, shaking my hand as if I was their best friend, when they actually know nothing about me except the name on my badge.'

'What about your parents?' she asked. 'Can you

bring them over for a visit?'

'I never thought of it,' he said, smiling slowly down at her, 'but I might. Why not?'

Of course, she knew there would be a moment of feeling bereft. It came immediately after she'd said goodbye to him and felt his eyes on her back as she walked out, smiling her good-nights to the courteous staff. But she also knew it was the last time she would see him and hoped he wouldn't be around in the morning. He was lovely.

After breakfast, the foyer was filled with the glorious warmth and sunshine she'd soon leave behind. She took a last look around the Christmas decorations and went upstairs to pack. Dad's photo went in the case last. She said to him, 'I did it, Dad, didn't I? I'm out in the world at last. I don't know how yet, but I'm going to do well and go far.'

The few English passengers climbed into the coach for the airport. Danielle sat on the hotel side, looked out of the window, and there was Marek, alone on the marble steps, hands in pockets, in checked shirt and jeans. He cocked his head and waved to her. She waved back, and tears came to her eyes. The driver pulled smoothly out into the sparkling landscape, along the road fringed with the purple-flowered bushes grown in red earth.

The Holy Family

The Holy Family

Shielding her eyes from the sun's early shimmer on the sea, Fiona glanced down at her once perfect swimsuit, then across at her sister's, probably bought for the occasion, impeccably tailored, with a pattern of large palm-leaves flattening her ample curves. They were sitting on the warm sand, taking a few moments before going in. The men were in the indoor pool with its added extras, but all the sisters wanted was the small basin of sea cupped in this quiet corner of the beach.

Fiona put on her swimming cap.

'What's that for?' asked Angela.

'I've washed my hair. We're going home today.'

'Oh, Fiona, we've got hours – the flight isn't until eight o'clock tonight. By the way, this was a great idea of yours to stay on for a few days after the wedding.'

'Yes. Peace at last, after all that eating and drinking and talking to people we haven't seen for years.'

Angela had no children but adored weddings. 'I loved every minute of it – Lisa's lip quivering as she repeated the words, Jamie, steady, looking lovingly down at her, the view over the sea from the gardens, international menu, wild dancing afterwards. All perfect. You did really well helping Lisa with the logistics. Must have been a nightmare setting all this up abroad.'

'Well, the last-minute change of venue was a bit of a challenge, but in the end they got what they wanted.'

'Are you OK? Something worrying you?'

'No, no. Just exhausted, that's all.'

'Come on. Let's get into that sea. You deserve it.'

It was cold at first but Fiona sank in, tasted the salt, allowed herself to be buoyed up to the surface and floated on her back. The movement of the waves washed away in an instant the anxiety of months. The sea was something she did not need to control. She rolled over and plunged her head under, cooling her face. Coming up for air she swam towards her sister.

'Isn't this bliss?' she said. 'The best moment of any holiday. And don't you sometimes think we've got everything wrong if I'm saying that? Seeing my daughter married should have been the best moment.'

'It was. She looked beautiful, and they're a

happy couple, going off to America on their trip. You can have a beach holiday any time.'

Fiona was not convinced. Swimming at this moment was better than anything she'd felt all the way through the massive fairy tale edifice of the wedding.

'You did well,' Angela said. 'You're an excellent mother, and probably soon you'll be a grandmother. They'll turn into a little family before long.'

Fiona didn't want to think ahead like this, certainly not now.

'Anyway, shall we get out?' said Angela. 'I told Campbell we'd see them on the sunbeds. We can go into the sea again over there.'

'You go, Angela. I'm going to stay in for five minutes. This will be my last swim. Tell Colin I'll be there soon.'

At the end of family holidays she'd always swum alone like this, cherishing the fun they'd had on yet another beach, looking back at the shore, alive with its busy goings-on. *Was* there something wrong with her? She'd been on the verge of tears quite a lot recently. It had been wonderful when Lisa announced their engagement, but ever since, she'd felt afraid to contact her, wanting to help and advise about the wedding but not interfere. She *had* been unhappy and now it was visible. She felt the pull of the current, swam with it for a while, then carefully timed her climb up the shifting sand between one thrashing wave and the next. She'd rather cope with struggles like this, she thought, than the endless effort of getting on in life. Couldn't we all live more simply? She shook sand from the towel, dried herself, and whispered goodbye to the sea.

The hotel lobby was empty. In her bathrobe she took the lift upstairs. The bedroom was cool and peaceful. She showered, put on shorts and T shirt, hung her swimsuit on the balcony. On the way out she returned the beach towel to the spa in the basement. I'm getting the hang of beach-life at last, she thought.

The glass doors of the hotel opened obligingly and she stepped out into the morning sun feeling calm and clean. People all wore flip-flops at the beach but this was the first pair she'd ever bought. They were bright red and unexpectedly comfortable. Now they were gently crunching over grains of sand across the waving shadow of a palm on the promenade. To the right, a delivery van's side pictured breads and pastries. Toddlers played on a slide while mums sat in the shady garden behind the van – for them it was a normal weekday before the start of the holiday season. She passed the beach restaurant on the left. Only two short rows of bright blue sunbeds had been put out on the beach.

On one of these cousin Barbara was awkwardly perched, dressed for the journey, and no doubt desperate to be relaxing on her sofa by the French windows at home in Dorking.

'So glad to catch you,' she said. 'We've only got until 10.30.' A few comments about the success of the wedding, then she was on to their new conservatory, their son's new job and traffic on the M25. The men were discussing the probable consequences of leaving the European Union. Barbara was moving on to gossip about other members of the family when, *Bap! Bap! Bap!* came the sound of a small hard ball hitting a wooden bat. Fiona knew and loved this sound. She smiled to herself remembering the pleasure of that beach pastime, thinking of the high scores she'd reached with her son. Usually at the water's edge, pairs of players would be laughing as they dropped the ball in the water and had to chase after it. This time the sound was coming from players quite close behind them.

'What a racket!' said Barbara. 'Why don't they play over there on that huge empty stretch of sand?'

'They've got a baby,' said Fiona. The baby started to cry.

'I don't know why people have children if they don't want to look after them,' said Barbara under her breath.

Fiona slanted her sunbed to be in the shade and

saw the young couple put their game away.

'Come on Lovely,' said Barbara's husband. 'Time to go home.'

Barbara lumbered into a standing position, dusted herself down. Profuse expressions of thanks, the women embracing, the men shaking hands, and then they were gone.

The sisters and their husbands agreed to have a proper lunch later at the beach restaurant, then settled, reading in absorbed silence in the shade, except for Angela who was sunbathing. African traders, with huge bundles of tablecloths, heaved their wares hopefully along the beach. Fiona looked back towards the striped encampment of the young family.

The baby sat up straight on the sunbed cradled around by his father's body. Trying to grasp a little spade, he was dignified and still, and reminded her of medieval paintings of the Virgin and Child in which the child is not a fat bouncing baby but a miniature man, sometimes wearing a crown, his hand held up in blessing. The father, slim and tanned, in red bathing shorts, bent his fair head, speaking quietly to his child in a language which was not Spanish. A slender girl equally tanned, appeared from behind their parasol and sat sideways behind the father leaning gently round to join in. The father peeled off the tiny blue and white T shirt over the baby's head, leaving just his plastic nappy.

The mother stood up, stretching and yawning in her yellow Lycra bikini, her figure perfectly restored after the birth, then walked round to their white sports bag where she found a packet of thin rice-crackers. They had one each, the baby too, turning his feathery head in concentration as he nibbled. Later, it was the girl who was sitting behind the child saying goodbye to the father as he prepared to leave. Fiona thought they could be lifeguards, fitting their shifts around their child, or a pair of fitness professionals on a short holiday-break.

It was a scene of wonder to her – the ease with which they attended equally to their baby, the absence of fuss with sun-cream, hats and toys, the way they kept the baby comfortable, allowing the three of them, for a short time, to be happy together on the beach. Bringing up children was no easier now than before but these young people seemed to be getting it right. Enough. She returned to her short story. When she next looked up the family had vanished.

The other three decided they needed to change before lunch. Fiona felt glad to be left by herself again. The beach stretched away empty. The waves were coming in calmer now. Suddenly she remembered holding her baby Lisa at the water's edge somewhere, her little face fearless, crying out with excitement, pointing at the waves. Here, unnoticed, the waves came in and were dragged back one after the other. She thought of the couple with their baby she'd just been watching. That little family was just beginning – hers was finished. Just thinking the word *finished,* made her eyes fill with tears. There was nobody there. She let them flow.

Warriors

Warriors

It was November, 1975. Judy Harris reached home after an awful day in school. On the way home in the Tube she'd felt more than ever the burden that teaching had suddenly put on her shoulders. Only last summer she'd been in a seminar room at London University presenting her postgraduate thesis in Linguistics and now she was trying to put across Shakespeare and English grammar to teenage girls who thought of school mainly as a place to see their friends. She might have to give it up.

She'd been telling her flatmate Steve how difficult it all was at the weekend.

'What did you expect?' Steve had said. 'You could at least have tried for a good school, rather than an East London comprehensive.' He was doing post-graduate study in Anthropology and was convinced that she'd made a mistake giving up academic life.

'I know. I do feel as if I've been dropped from a great height,' she said, 'but I needed a job. I'm 24. I can't study for ever. There's a teacher shortage, so they wanted me. With a good English degree, I'm employed on probation, without Teacher Training.'

'That's even worse.' They'd laughed, and she'd said that really she had no idea how to teach.

'What about that book you've been reading over the summer?'

'Oh yes. Lots of advice about the classroom, but all I can remember is that you should never smile until Christmas.'

'Why not?'

'Because the students mustn't think you are their *friend.* They need to respect you.'

'And after Christmas?' Steve asked, prepared to nod respectfully.

'Only smile a bit.'

She put down her heavy bag in the corridor. No one home. The kitchen was cold. Bacon fat had solidified in the frying pan and dirty dishes covered the table. She and Steve were the only two left of the initial crowd of flatmates. He owned the flat. His parents in Australia had bought it for him. She waited for the kettle to boil, staring out on a dull, colourless scene, sky and buildings competing for lifelessness, until the steam obliterated the lot. Gripping her mug of hot tea in one hand with the bag in the other, she navigated the steep steps up to her room where she switched on the electric fire.

Sipping the tea, she emptied the bag on the floor, intending a confrontation with everything that had gone wrong in the day. A bad start. Too late to catch the bus, she'd stood all the way on the tube which made her even more tired than usual for a Monday. With horror she'd remembered it was her Assembly Duty. This involved rounding up girls trying to hide. She found five final-year girls in the toilets. They tried this on every single day and sometimes got away with it.

'You know perfectly well that you must go to Assembly. Now go on!' she'd told them.

Silence, as they sensed her failure and worked out how to play it. 'Look at her skirt,' one said to a second.

'Are you a new teacher?' asked a third.

'Never mind what I am. Will you just go to Assembly!' Nothing happened. The girls just stared back at her.

'Right! Give me your names and I'll report you to the Headmistress.'

'Miss, our Form Teacher lets us stay in the classroom instead of Assembly because we've got our exams this year,' said the fourth girl.

'Not true. I'll have your names please.' Judy realised the futility of this threat as they could see she had no pen and paper. They didn't know who she was and didn't respect her authority. This battle was lost.

'Do what you like,' she'd muttered, and left them. Coming towards her was Mrs Richards, Head of History. Not wanting to admit failure, she'd let her pass, exchanging only a smile with this competent teacher, who could then be heard from inside the toilets issuing a brief and friendly instruction, with instant success. Giggling, the girls had scuttled past Judy on the bridge to the Assembly Hall.

After this, on the way to the classroom for Lesson 1, dread of the day turned into physical nausea and a longing to be anywhere but here on this Monday morning. She'd managed to pull herself together enough to open the door with an appearance of composure to face 2B, but then what happened in that lesson had seriously upset her.

The front door banged. That would be Steve. Thank goodness, she thought, and went downstairs. Steve was kicking off his muddy boots. You could always depend on Steve to discuss anything whatsoever.

'Any tea?' he asked.

'I'll make you some,' she said, putting the kettle on and clearing a space on the table. 'How was your day? Discovered any new tribes?'

He sat down. 'All right, I suppose,' he said, handing her a typed sheet from his bag. 'I thought you'd be interested in this lecture tonight on your specialism. Would you like to come with me?'

Judy read the title: *New Departures in Anthropological Linguistics.* 'I think I'd like that,' she said. 'It'll take my mind off school.'

'Why? What's up? No improvement? I don't know how you do it. Admit it – you must be missing your old life.'

'Yes, and I'd be happy to re-visit it tonight.' She put his tea on the table. 'What about you? Have you had any more thoughts about what you'll do next year?'

'There may be a junior post in the department, or I might go and study back home. There's plenty of research going on in the Pacific Islands.'

Steve had never had money worries. Pacific Islands! She inserted him into a Gauguin painting, lazing among dark-skinned beauties on a beach. 'Shall I make us a sandwich?' she asked.

'Good idea. We'll leave in an hour. You know, Judy, you could come with me on my fieldwork. You did so well in your Linguistic Theory. You could study the language while I look at the kinship.'

Buttering the bread, she laughed, picturing herself all alone in their rough shack with her Polynesian dictionary while he interviewed the beauties about their mothers and uncles. Relationship-wise, Steve was on a break after a long series of girlfriends moving in and out of the flat. 'Cheese?' she asked, opening the fridge. 'Tell you what. I don't think I want to go there to study, but I'd love to come and visit you.'

Judy took the sandwich up to eat in her room. Now, thankfully, there was only a short time left to worry about tomorrow. From the messy bag-contents on the floor, she picked up 2B's homework sheets and replayed the awful lesson in her head. They'd talked all the way through the register, catching up with weekend gossip and she'd tolerated this only because she was buoyed up, anticipating a bumper harvest of homework. Why? Because during their previous lesson they'd been silent for the first time, listening to a story called *The Last Witch.* She'd led a good discussion afterwards, then set what she thought was easy homework.

'Right, 2B. That's enough talking,' she'd said. 'Can I have the homework on your desks please.'

They had done this in an eerie silence. Instead of the one page she'd asked for, neatly copied out in pen, there were half pages, quarter pages, some with crossings-out, some in pencil, several dog-eared and quite a few not there at all. She'd lost her temper out of sheer disappointment.

'This homework is absolutely disgraceful,' she'd shouted. 'I want you all to come to detention after school today to do it again.'

'No, Miss. You can't do that,' they'd clamoured indignantly. 'Our parents will wonder where we are.'

No one had turned up. Instead of clarifying the

rules right away with Mrs Dunlop, the Head of House, she'd decided to leave it until the next day.

'Time to go, Judy,' Steve shouted from downstairs.'

Judy jumped up to get her coat. She'd re-pack for Tuesday when she got home.

They took their seats in the lecture room of the Royal Anthropological Institute. It smelt of old wood and dust. The floorboards and chairs creaked as people came in, talking in a whisper as if in a holy place. On the walls were oil paintings of the founding fathers of anthropology interspersed with bronze busts of 'natives' labelled with their tribe and habitat. The globe in one corner and Evolution of Man chart in the other indicated that the study of indigenous peoples was a scientific one and not mere travellers' tales. A grey-haired old man in a tweed jacket approached the podium followed by a younger man. The low hum of conversation subsided.

Judy felt comfortable and relaxed. Normal adult behaviour. No one was going to get up out of their seat and insult the speaker or start chattering while he spoke. Professor Andrews had studied a tribe in the highlands of New Guinea during many visits over forty years, living with them, learning and using their language. The slide projector clicked, showing the earliest coloured engravings of warriors in battle regalia, running at their enemy with spears, then up-to-date photos of young tribesmen prepared for an initiation ceremony, painted in the traditional red, yellow and white designs. Judy admired the courage of anthropological 'fieldworkers' like him, striving to understand these living examples of 'pre-civilized' societies, but when, at the end of his interesting factual section, the professor began explaining how you could look at ethnic languages in terms of modern linguistic theory, she turned off. Surely, knowing the people as intimately as he did, he could have thought of a better way of helping them. What would they think if they were here in the room? He'd said that their way of life was now under threat. How many government officials in New Guinea, she wondered, would know enough of what he knew to help them adapt? She didn't even know why she was thinking like this.

Normally, at the end of such a lecture, she would have been having that stage-fright feeling before asking a question. Venerable turtle-heads would have twisted slowly round to see who she was. Now that she was an ex-student, nobody would be interested, and she would probably cause a few heart attacks if she spoke up. Only a couple of timid points of scholarly clarification were raised by the audience.

On the way home on the bus, Judy felt sad she

could no longer voice her ideas like she used to. 'I don't think much of these new theories,' she said to Steve. 'It's a narrow field which gets you nowhere.'

'Academics always burrow onwards in their own fields. Most of it isn't useful, just interesting.'

Judy felt she had known this all along but only admitted it now. 'I want to be useful,' she said. 'Also, I need to be active, talking, not sitting thinking all day.'

'OK, Judy, you might be right. Give teaching a year and see how it goes.'

First thing on Tuesday morning, she clarified the detention rules with Mrs Dunlop, her Head of House, who also kindly filled her in on the circumstances of the girls who had defaulted on the homework: two had special needs and the third was having difficulties at home. Judy resolved to pay more attention to these girls in class, go round and help them when she'd set a written exercise.

2B were attentive at the beginning of class. She explained that they had been right about the detention, but she hoped there would be no need for it, that they would make a fresh start and try harder. Tuesday was English grammar. She had to teach adverbs, the ones ending in *-ly,* and felt this had to be brightened up somehow. She got them to guess an adverb that she acted out, then come out and do their own for the class. This did become a bit noisy, but they liked it. She gave them homework which was even easier than the last time.

Travelling home that day, she reflected that there *was* help out there for her if she asked for it. Her Head of Department had briefed her at the beginning of the year about the curriculum and textbooks, although warning her not to expect too much, and saying she herself would be retiring in July. The English Inspector had observed her first year class and seemed pleased enough.

The next week, 2B's homework was better, and she gave special help to the girls identified by the Head of House.

One Monday morning in December, being short of time, she'd put on the clothes she'd been wearing on Saturday night, which had a much more feminine look than her prim and neat 'teacher' outfits. A difficult class of older girls had suddenly softened, become nicer, and one volunteered, 'Like your top, Miss.' Perhaps she'd been wearing too much armour.

During the rest of the Christmas term, she no longer felt at war with the girls but nevertheless had to be a warrior every day, striving to understand where they were coming from and how to interest them.

One evening, she tidied the kitchen properly before Steve got home.

'You look happy,' he said.

'I've just had a look at my bank statement,' she said. 'Three times as much money as I used to have, and I've been too busy to spend any. Do you fancy a curry? I'll treat you.'

Steve was happy to oblige. Over the lamb biriyani, she told him that things were looking up, that she'd had a letter from the English Inspector to say they would be sending her on a course to update her on new methods of teaching English. He said he'd applied for a research post in Canberra, but he'd miss their curries.

The end of term was approaching. The girls were getting restless. She dreaded the last day, couldn't conceive of letting classes just sit and chatter. She asked Mrs Dunlop what she usually did to keep them occupied.

'I give out word-searches and other easy word-puzzles' she said. They love these.'

2B would be the worst. She ran off some carbon copies of puzzles on the Banda machine to be going on with. Then at the beginning of the lesson, a better idea came to her which might work.

Near the top of the blackboard, she wrote: *Miss Harris Sings.*

They were all eyes. 'Are you going to sing to us, Miss?'

'Yes I am.' Looking around to make sure they were ready, she said. ' I'm going to sing you a traditional Scottish song. It's called ' *The Bonnie*

Banks of Loch Lomond.'

She just about remembered the words. Clapping and cheering, they wanted more. 'Another one, Miss!'

'Wait a second,' she said, turned to the board and at the top wrote *Talent Show*, put a 1 in front of 'Miss Harris Sings' and numbers 2-10 down the left side, telling them they were all in the show, and needed to put their names in the spaces, in groups or solo. There was a moment of disbelief, then she saw them come to life. 'Come out and put your names down when you're ready,' she said.

Sitting at her desk correcting exercise-books, she heard them get organised.

'You've got your violin, haven't you?' said somebody, while others got into huddles, whispering about which of their favourite pop-songs they could do. 'Yeah, do your imitations,' said another, and 'Where's that poem we read?'

Just to be on the safe side, Judy wrote at number 7, 'Miss Harris sings again.' Soon there were ten acts written up, all in different handwriting.

She couldn't believe the hidden talent that suddenly burst out that morning. Two girls, normally resistant to her teaching, sang a song from the charts which they knew by heart, perfectly in tune. The whole lesson was spent smiling and clapping. For Judy, a huge gulf had been bridged.

She'd made it to the end of term. It would be hard work, probably with many more battles, but not winning or losing, just doing your best. As she walked out of the gate that day, she realised she was smiling. It was Christmas, so that was OK.

The Visitor

The Visitor

When I got home the phone was ringing. I dropped my handbag and the supermarket bag at the door, skidded across my parquet floor and got it in time. Nicole sounded anxious.

'Diana, is that you? Listen – I haven't got long. It's about Cheryl. She's in a bad state.'

'What do you mean?' I asked, slumping on to my new sofa.

'I mean *depressed*. I went up to see her last week. From what I can see she's not her old self any more.'

'None of us is.'

'She's stuck out there in the country all on her own, doing nothing. Trouble is, it's as if she doesn't even *realise* she's depressed.'

'Hang on a minute. Last I heard, she had a husband.'

'She does, but he's never there. I didn't even see him. Look, do you think you could go up there and visit, see what you think?'

'I haven't seen her for ten years – we don't even send Christmas cards any more.'

'She'd love to see you. We talked about you, how well your new job is going. Don't you sometimes have to travel up that way?'

'Yes. I'm going up next month, so I suppose I could drop in and see her.'

Nicole sounded relieved and gave me Cheryl's number and address.

On the day of the visit, the Norwich conference finished after lunch. I'd booked to stay that night in the hotel where the Conference was held rather than rush back to London. It was time to go and find Cheryl's place. I put the details into the SAT NAV and it said 45 minutes.

I put the roof down and took my time, rolling between barley fields, threading through silent villages, but half an hour later, the wooden road-signs had disappeared from the T junctions and the woman in the SAT NAV said *'Make a U turn,'* just once too often, so I switched her off. For some reason I didn't want to get on my mobile and ask Cheryl. Anyway there were no landmarks. I drove until there was a village, pulled in and knocked on the door of the first house. The old boy pointed me in the right direction after explaining in his Norfolk accent that during the war a lot of signs had been removed so the American troops would never know exactly where they were, and had never been put back.

I turned on Radio 2 to re-connect with the normal world. The car lurched along narrow roads full of pot-holes and finally there was a small hidden entrance on the left, with a sign *'Briar Cottage'* almost completely hidden by a wild-rose bush. I turned into a winding sandy lane ending with an isolated brick cottage.

I parked on a bare patch of the scrubby grass and in my high heels crunched to the front door on a rough pebble path. I rang the bell and waited.

'Diana!' A beaming middle-aged woman in old clothes with unbrushed hair hugged me warmly, held my narrow shoulders and sized me up. 'Yes, it's still you. You look so smart. And just look at your car!'

'I don't feel so smart,' I said. 'Sorry I'm late. Got lost.'

'Don't worry. You're here now.' She showed me the bathroom and we agreed tea could wait until later.

Her lounge had whitewashed walls, bare floorboards and worn chintz- covered sofa and chairs. 'So you're up on business? What business is there out here?' she asked.

'Food-production,' I told her. 'Chickens. I've been to our annual conference in Norwich today. I run a national training company for staff. There's a lot to learn now with the hygiene regulations for free-range birds.' I stopped there as my old school friend looked a bit out of her depth, and made a funny face to reassure her, 'Don't worry, I don't have anything to do with *actual* chickens, so never mind all that, I'm here to see you.'

'Well,' she said, 'we've got a few hours at least to catch up. It's been so long. Where do we start? You know, this is ridiculous, but the face you made when you said *actual chickens* just now made me think of something way back in the past.'

'Really? What?' I asked.

'It was that time in the gym – when you couldn't remember the country dance steps you made that face.' Cheryl tried to stop herself laughing. 'What was her name, that teacher?'

'Shorty Mac Dermot!' I suddenly remembered, and we were both laughing uncontrollably.

'Because,' she spluttered, 'she wore these *long shorts!'* We gave in to our laughter, blowing our noses between bursts.

Cheryl recovered first. 'We must have been awful to teach. We were so rebellious. Remember that night we got locked out and had to ring the emergency bell?'

'God, yes, the terrible three. Our parents had to be summoned. And they were *paying* for all this. We did get a very good education though.'

Cheryl was happily musing about the past but I wanted to get her talking about the present. I went over to the antique side table and picked up a silver-framed wedding photo.

'So, Cheryl, I said, 'is this the good-looking man you married? Men with long hair, mm. Blonde as well.'

'Yes, that's Paul. He was so handsome. Still is, and he's kept the long hair-style. I met him almost as soon as I came out here to stay with mummy. He was working on her house. He specializes in period buildings. He seemed so sensible and grounded in his craft. You know why I left London don't you?'

'I only know that you hated it.'

'It was my first job, drawing for that fashion magazine. It was fine, but suddenly I was in this relationship with the boss, which I thought was true love. Turned out he went through all new recruits, made a point of it. My whole life collapsed when he dropped me. I was so naïve, but the damage was done. I just ran from it and from the whole fake London scene.'

'Must have been a very bad shock to make you decide to come all the way out here.'

'It was, but everything was so calm and wholesome.'

She was right about that. From the window we could see nothing but leafy branches against blue sky.

'The pace was slow – I felt I could recover here,' she said.

I replaced the photo. On the opposite wall hung

a large oil-painting of a nude on a Moroccan bedspread. I went up and examined it. 'This is a lovely piece of work. It's yours isn't it?'

She nodded. 'It's from art school days,' she said.

'You were so talented at school. Did you get more of a chance to paint out here?'

'Yes. I tried to keep it up. I've done a few life-classes, but it's hard to sell your work. People seem to prefer pictures of haystacks or places they know.'

I pressed on. 'OK, so you and Paul bought this house together?'

'It was Paul's family home. Mummy helped by buying his father out and he went to live in a smaller place.'

'Paul's business must be thriving. I saw so many timbered houses on the way from Norwich.'

'Oh, yes. He's never had to advertise. It's all word of mouth around here.'

'And what about you? Did you take up any country crafts?'

'Not crafts. I did do a course in massage but couldn't find many customers. Don't forget I was bringing up Fergus for all these years.'

'Of course. How old is he now?'

'He's 19. He lives in Norwich. Works in insurance. Doing well. Comes to see us now and again.'

Cheryl took me for a walk round the garden. I

followed her, picking my way over the uneven turf past derelict out-buildings, tripping up occasionally in my high heels. We stopped to look at an overgrown vegetable patch. 'We grow our own vegetables. We did quite well for a while but since I've had my bad knee I just can't dig any more.'

'That's a pity,' I said. 'What treatment have you had for it?'

'I used to see an osteopath but it got too expensive.'

'And doesn't Paul help? I thought most country people could turn their hand to basic gardening.'

'Not builders it seems.'

I sat at a rough table with wobbly legs, while Cheryl made tea. It was served in two cracked mugs without even the suggestion of a cake.

'You must see your mother a lot. She lives quite nearby doesn't she?' I asked.

'No. She used to, but not long after I came back she re-married and moved to Kent. She does visit, but I don't go there much.'

'I see, but you've probably got people you know in the village?'

'When Fergus was at school, there were some mums I got to know but I don't see them any more, except one, who takes me to the cinema or a concert in Norwich.'

'*Takes* you? Does that mean you don't have a car?'

'No, I do. We usually go in hers, that's all.'

'And you and Paul probably go out as a couple.'

'Not now. In the beginning I used to hang around the pub with him and his crowd. There was a lot of drinking. I just got bored with it. We do our own thing. He doesn't care for culture, and I don't care for agricultural shows. Look, he works hard all day, gets home late and at the weekend just wants to rest. I cook him an enormous roast on Sundays.'

I pictured her clearing up every Sunday in that dismal kitchen while he put his feet up. I heard her go on about how clever he was to source nearly all their food from people he knew. This may be a lost cause, I thought. Is she deep-down quite happy with her country lifestyle?' Am I going to leave her to it?

But as she began to go through the details of where each of the food items came from, I lost interest and was thinking back on our threesome. That was where we got our determination to stand up for ourselves, to make our own choices in life, become what we wanted to be. Cheryl had been the loving and binding force, pulling Nicole and I together. Now Nicole and I were the ones doing OK and Cheryl, well, she was shipwrecked, wasn't she? I missed how we could all laugh together. I missed her dreamy appreciation of the world, her eye for beauty, how attractive she used to look in whatever she put on, mostly from charity shops.

She was in the middle of how they sourced their meat from Paul's cousin's farm-shop. I looked over to the ex-vegetable patch. A solitary Azalea stood in the corner, recently planted, but its pink petals were darkening and its leaves already turning brown. The soil wasn't right for it – the poor thing was drying out, fighting for its life.

Cheryl looked at me enquiringly as I suddenly stood up. 'Right,' I said. 'I'm taking you out for dinner. Where can we go?'

It was as if I'd made a preposterous suggestion. 'No, it's OK, Diana, really. I've got my veggie stew left over from last night. There's plenty.'

I tried another tack. 'Cheryl, let's go out. I'd love to see a proper country pub.'

This seemed to please her. 'All right, if you like. The local pub is fine,' she said. 'We can go in your car. Paul's got mine. His truck's being repaired. It's always at the garage these days. I can write a note telling him where we've gone and where his dinner is. Let me just get changed.' She bounded upstairs.

I went into the bathroom to freshen up and when I came out she was standing in the kitchen in a cotton dress and sandals. Her hair was brushed and she'd put on red lipstick. I smiled and said how nice she looked.

In my car, a pop song dating from our time in London was playing on the radio. We hummed along at first then joined in at the top of our voices all the way to the pub. 'I'm so pleased you came, Diana. Let's keep in touch,' Cheryl said as we arrived.

The pub was a dark hive humming with Friday evening drinkers. Heads turned as we came in. I was smartly dressed but hadn't expected to be noticed. In London nobody notices anybody. Cheryl stopped to speak to someone she knew, so I made my way through an arch to the almost empty restaurant area. I chose a little round table.

It was quite early and there was only one couple sitting in the last booth at the far-end. The man had his arm around a young woman who was gazing into his eyes. He bent forward and kissed her, a curtain of his long fair hair hiding their faces. When he looked up I recognised Paul from the wedding photo.

Cheryl came through the arch, saw me first, then them, turned on her heels and made for the door. I went after her through the crowds and into the car park where she stood limply holding my car door handle. I thought she might faint, so I put my arm around her shoulders. 'Time to go,' I said, opening the door for her. I didn't know where, but I knew I was going to help her towards wherever it was.

ACKNOWLEDGEMENTS

Thanks are due to my husband Maurice for encouraging me to publish these stories and putting up with the consequences. Thank you to our son David for laying out the file for publication, and to our daughter Louise for help with the cover design. Thank you to close family who commented after reading or listening to stories – Louise, Stewart, Graham, Jill, and friends, Barrie, Penny, Eve, Sue, Vanessa, Pam, also to my final proof-readers – Louise, Maurice, Robyn, Sophie, Christine and Mary Anne.

I am grateful to Writers' Centre Norwich (now the National Centre for Writing) for the many Creative Writing workshops I attended over the last five years, and also for the one-to-one encouragement I received recently through coaching with Heidi Williamson and mentoring with Katri Skala.

Printed in Great Britain
by Amazon